3 2894 00161 1126

W9-BDQ-244

NO LONGER THE PROPERTY OF
EAST GREENWICH FREE LIBRARY

For — who else? —
Mark and Lawrence. CF

To Robert and the two Erics,
Eric and Erik. LM

Text copyright © 2010 by Cary Fagan
Illustrations copyright © 2010 by Luc Melanson
Published in Canada and the USA in 2010 by Groundwood Books

All rights reserved. No part of this publication may be reproduced,
stored in a retrieval system or transmitted, in any form or by any
means, without the prior written consent of the publisher or a
license from The Canadian Copyright Licensing Agency (Access
Copyright). For an Access Copyright license, visit
www.accesscopyright.ca or call toll free to 1-800-893-5777.

Groundwood Books / House of Anansi Press
110 Spadina Avenue, Suite 801, Toronto, Ontario M5V 2K4
or c/o Publishers Group West
1700 Fourth Street, Berkeley, CA 94710

We acknowledge for their financial support of our publishing
program the Canada Council for the Arts, the Government of Canada
through the Canada Book Fund (CBF) and the Ontario Arts Council.

Canada Council **Conseil des Arts**
for the Arts **du Canada**

ONTARIO ARTS COUNCIL
CONSEIL DES ARTS DE L'ONTARIO

Library and Archives Canada Cataloguing in Publication
Fagan, Cary
Book of big brothers / Cary Fagan ; Luc Melanson, illustrator.
ISBN 978-0-88899-977-1
I. Melanson, Luc II. Title.
PS8561.A375B66 2010   jC813'.54   C2010-900591-0

Design by Michael Solomon
The illustrations are digital.
Printed and bound in China

BOOK OF
BIG
BROTHERS

Cary Fagan

pictures by
Luc Melanson

GROUNDWOOD BOOKS | HOUSE OF ANANSI PRESS | TORONTO BERKELEY

WHEN I WAS A LITTLE KID, I wasn't very big. But
I dreamed that I was a superhero, a detective, a
rock star on stage with my guitar. Sometimes
I was just a kid on a sinking ship who bravely
had to help people onto the lifeboats.

I daydreamed so much that on the way
home from school I would forget to look where
I was going.

Suddenly, I would be lost.

But my brothers always found me.

This is me when I was one week old. My brothers were waiting eagerly on the porch when my parents brought me home from the hospital. They argued over who got to hold me first.

"I want to hold him!" said my biggest brother.

"No, I do!" said my middle brother.

They dropped me.

I didn't break. I didn't even cry.

You know what I did?

I smiled.

At least that's what my brothers say. I don't remember.

When I was in the first grade, three sisters named Martha, Annie and Fran started to pick on me. They called me "Short Pants" and "Mop Head." They picked up rotten pears and threw them at me. When I started to run, they chased me.

One day my brothers were waiting. They leapt out from behind the bushes, howling at the top of their lungs.

The sisters ran away. They never chased me again.

Martha gave me a card on Valentine's Day.

When I got sick with the measles, I had to stay home from school.

At recess time I could hear the kids shouting in the school yard. The afternoon dragged on and on. It felt like the whole world had forgotten me.

At last the school bell rang. Ten minutes later my brothers burst into the room.

"We will now perform a play called *The Pirate Baby*," they announced.

For the baby they used the neighbor's dog. It was the funniest thing I ever saw in my life.

But things weren't always good between us.

For his birthday, my middle brother got a plastic model kit of a monster called The Creature from the Black Lagoon. It was scary. At night I imagined the Creature crawling down from the dresser, sneaking into my room and climbing up the leg of my bed.

So I hired my big brother. I gave him one dollar.

He took the Creature into the garage and smashed it up with a hammer.

Boy, was my middle brother angry.

I think he's still mad about it.

We had lots of pets. Mice, rats, guinea pigs, hamsters and many, many fish. We even had rabbits. I guess the cage we built wasn't very secure because they were always getting out. I would look out the window in the morning and see my mother in her nightgown chasing the rabbits across the backyard.

But the pet I remember best was a green lizard. Now this is a sad story, so skip this page if you want to. I remember the lizard best because I killed it.

My brothers took it out onto the grass without telling me. Green lizard ... green grass. I stepped on it. Then I ran upstairs to my parents and burst into tears.

We held a funeral for the lizard. My brothers put their arms around me. That made me feel a little better.

One day I watched my brothers doing something in the school yard. They were bending down, staring at the gravel and picking something up. When I went over to them, they hid whatever they had.

After a week they finally showed me an old sock full of what they had collected. Tiny bits of gold.

"We're rich," my middle brother said.

"You didn't help us, so you don't get any," my big brother said.

I was so mad that I stomped my feet all the way home. I stomped up the porch steps and into the kitchen. I told my mother everything. It wasn't fair! I wanted to be rich too.

"They're teasing you," my mother said as she brought me a glass of milk and a plate of cookies. "It's only iron pyrite. Fool's gold. It isn't worth anything."

Wasn't that mean of them?

My brothers are pretty smart. But not all the time.

On Victoria Day, my big brother got some firecrackers from a friend. My middle brother got the idea of lighting them and throwing them into the hollow tree in our neighbor's backyard. I just tagged along.

The firecrackers made a terrific noise.

And then smoke started pouring out of the hole.

The tree was on fire!

The man next door called the fire department. The fire truck came screaming up the street. The firefighters, in their big boots and coats, put a hose into the hole and put out the fire.

Our parents took the television away. And dessert. We had to cut our neighbor's grass for a month.

I got punished too, but I didn't complain. I was glad they didn't put us in jail!

Here's another dumb thing we did. Played football inside the house when our parents were out.

My big brother threw the ball. My middle brother leapt up to intercept the pass. The ball bounced out of my hands and knocked over a little porcelain woman playing a harp.

Our parents had brought it back from their honeymoon in Italy or some place like that.

The little porcelain woman fell to the rug. Her arm broke off.

"Look what you did!"

"I didn't do it. You did it!"

Carefully my big brother glued the arm back and returned the little porcelain woman to the table. We never said a word to our mom and dad.

So please don't tell them.

All of a sudden my brothers became very interested in where babies come from. At school, they had heard strange rumors. So our parents sat us down and explained all about it.

I didn't listen. No, thank you. Instead, I built a robot out of blocks. It was the best robot I ever built.

One summer night we made a tent in the backyard by draping an old sheet over the clothesline and pegging the ends into the ground. We begged our parents until they agreed to let us stay in it all night.

We lay in our sleeping bags, pillows under our heads, and read comic books by flashlight. At last we turned off the light to go to sleep. From somewhere came the sound of a car pulling into a driveway. Then a single chirp of a bird. Then silence.

Suddenly, there was a terrible growling. "Grrr … grrr …"

Something was scratching at the side of the tent trying to get in!

My big brother screamed. My middle brother screamed. They fumbled for the flashlight. At last my big brother turned it on.

It was … me!

"I knew it all along," said my older brother.

"Me too," said my middle brother.

Then they hit me with their pillows.

After camping in the backyard, my brothers decided that we should ride our banana bikes to the Rocky Mountains.

We packed chocolate bars, bags of chips, and apple juice. We took sweaters, a change of underwear and two weeks' allowance.

Saturday morning came. We got up early. Put on our knapsacks. Got our bikes out of the garage. And started to roll.

We were halfway down the driveway when our mother called out from the house.

"And just where do you think you're going?"

We went to the park instead.

My brothers and I are getting older. Sometimes we get along and sometimes we don't. But there are still a lot of things we want to do together.

Like build a raft.

And dig a tunnel from our house to the candy store.

And climb the Rocky Mountains.

After all, they're only two thousand miles away.

East Greenwich Free Library

3 2894 00161 1126

NO LONGER THE PROPERTY OF
EAST GREENWICH FREE LIBRARY

E
FAG

East Greenwich Free Library

NO LONGER THE PROPERTY OF
EAST GREENWICH FREE LIBRARY

DEMCO